Dear Parents,

Welcome to the Scholastic Reader series. We have taken over 80 years of experience with teachers, parents, and children and put it into a program that is designed to match your child's interests and skills.

Level 1— Short sentences and stories made up of words kids can sound out using their phonics skills and words that are important to remember.

Level 2— Longer sentences and stories with words kids need to know and new "big" words that they will want to know.

Level 3— From sentences to paragraphs to longer stories, these books have large "chunks" of texts and are made up of a rich vocabulary.

Level 4— First chapter books with more words and fewer pictures.

It is important that children learn to read well enough to succeed in school and beyond. Here are ideas for reading this book with your child:

- Look at the book together. Encourage your child to read the title and make a prediction about the story.
- Read the book together. Encourage your child to sound out words when appropriate. When your child struggles, you can help by providing the word.
- Encourage your child to retell the story. This is a great way to check for comprehension.
- Have your child take the fluency test on the last page to check progress.

Scholastic Readers are designed to support your child's efforts to learn how to read at every age and every stage. Enjoy helping your child learn to read and love to read.

— **Francie Alexander**
   Chief Education Officer
   Scholastic Education

For Reed
—D.M.

Text copyright © 1998 by David McPhail.
Illustrations copyright © 1998 by David McPhail.
Activities copyright © 2003 Scholastic Inc.

All rights reserved. Published by Scholastic Inc.
SCHOLASTIC, CARTWHEEL BOOKS, and associated logos are trademarks
and/or registered trademarks of Scholastic Inc.

Library of Congress Cataloging-in-Publication Data is available.

ISBN 0-590-84910-7

19 18   09 10 11 12/0
Printed in the U.S.A.   109
First printing, January 1998

The Day the Sheep Showed Up

by David McPhail

Scholastic Reader — Level 2

Cartwheel
·B·O·O·K·S·®

SCHOLASTIC INC.
New York Toronto London Auckland Sydney
Mexico City New Delhi Hong Kong Buenos Aires

One day when the barnyard
animals woke up, they saw
something strange.

"I wonder what it is,"
said the duck.

"It's white like you,"
said the goose.
"Maybe it's a duck."

"BAAAAA!" went the strange animal. "I'm not a duck, or a goose, a pig, a cow, a rooster, or a dog. I'm a sheep!"

"You mean like
the goose and me?"
asked the duck.

"We both have webbed feet,"
said the goose, "but I honk
and he quacks."

"Exactly," said the sheep,
"or like the pig and the dog.
They each have four legs."

"But he likes mud,"
said the dog,
"and I don't."

And you and I both eat clover. But I have a long tail and yours is short.

"But we are all
barnyard animals,"
the sheep reminded them.

For a moment,
all of the animals were silent.

Then the dog spoke.
"Do you like to play games?"

"Like tag?"
said the goose.

"Or hide-and-seek?"
said the pig.

"I love to play games,"
said the sheep.
"Can we play one now?"

"Sure," said the goose.
"Tag! You're it!"

The sheep laughed
and chased the
other animals.

All morning they played,
until they got so tired
they decided to rest.

"You get tired just as we do,"
the duck told the sheep.

"Exactly the same,"
replied the sheep.